A
FIRE IN
MY HEAD

Ben Okri was born in Minna, Nigeria. His childhood was divided between Nigeria, where he saw first hand the consequences of war, and London. He has won many prizes over the years for his fiction, and is also an acclaimed essayist, playwright, and poet. In 2019 *Astonishing the Gods* was named as one of the BBC's '100 Novels That Shaped Our World'.

Also by Ben Okri

A
FIRE IN
MY HEAD

Poems for the Dawn

BEN OKRI

HEAD
ZEUS

An Apollo Book

First published in the UK in 2021 by Head of Zeus Ltd
This paperback edition first published in the UK in 2022 by Head of Zeus Ltd,
part of Bloomsbury Publishing Plc

9 7 5 3 1 2 4 6 8

A catalogue record for this book is available from
the British Library.

ISBN (PB): 9781803281285
ISBN (E): 9781800242999

Typeset by Adrian McLaughlin

Printed and bound in Great Britain by
CPI Group (UK) Ltd, Croydon CR0 4YY

MIX
Paper from
responsible sources
FSC® C171272

Head of Zeus Ltd
First Floor East
5–8 Hardwick Street
London EC1R 4RG

WWW.HEADOFZEUS.COM

A
FIRE IN
MY HEAD

Material in this collection has previously appeared as follows:

'Finding the Present' was featured in Eli Strik's exhibition, 'In Search of the Present', at the Espoo Museum of Modern Art (EMMA) in Finland in 2016. 'A Shakespeare Portrait' was first published in the *Financial Times* in 2014. 'Notre-Dame is Telling Us Something' was broadcast on BBC Radio 4 on 26 April, 2019. 'A New Dream of Politics' was published in the *Guardian* on 12 October, 2015. 'closed, still open' was read by Ben Okri and filmed for the Coronet Theatre on 9 April, 2020. 'The Unknown Hour' was published in the *New Statesman* on 16 December, 2017. 'everest' was read aloud by Ben Fogle when he climbed Everest in July 2018, and featured in Ben Fogle's book, *Up: My Life's Journey to the Top of Everest* (2018). 'convergence' was read at the Zamyn festival at Tate Modern in 2013. 'Obama' was published in the *Guardian* on 19 January, 2017. 'a broken song' appeared in the *Guardian* on 21 October 1995 under the title 'For Ken Saro-Wiwa'. 'The Insider' was made into a short film of the same title by Mitra Tabrizian in 2018. 'Amnesty at Forty' was published in Amnesty global magazine in 2001. 'history of new forms' was printed in *David Hammons: Give me a moment* (2016) which accompanied the exhibition of the same name. 'revelations of saint time' featured on the wall of Grace Wells Bonner's exhibition, 'A Time For New Dreams', at the Serpentine Gallery in Spring 2019. 'cosmosis' was recorded as a song by Tony Allen, Remi Kabaka, and Damon Albarn in 2020. 'mother dance', 'dance of the new born', and 'ballet of the unseen' accompanied a dance-drama choreographed by Charlotte Jarvis at Dance Base as part of the Edinburgh International Festival in August 2019. 'shaved head poem' was published in *Adda*, the Commonwealth magazine on 18 June, 2020. 'Diallo's Testament' was commissioned by the National Portrait Gallery in 2013. 'invocation for the shrine 4' was featured on the wall of Grace Wells Bonner's exhibition, 'A Time For New Dreams', at the Serpentine Gallery in 2019. 'Grenfell Tower, June 2017' was published in the *Financial Times* on 23 June, 2017.

I went out to the hazel wood,
because a fire was in my head.

W. B. Yeats

CONTENTS

Read slowly

Unknown Hour

FINDING THE PRESENT

An extract

The present moment began with fire
And still it burns; it began with water,
And still they drown on the margins of Europe.
It began with air – see how they flee, see
How the bombs fall on houses made of sand,
Dreams made of flesh, the blind drones
Of remote war. But it began with earth,
Where all destinies are one, but many perish
For want of justice or soap or flowers
Instead of fears. Our age is confused:
The world runs ahead while humanity
Falls behind, trampled on by juggernauts
Whose names are the fearsome powers.
Across borders and nations, a new web
Of chains within the greatest horizons
The world has ever known. Water itself
Resists oppression. Press her down too much
And she erupts with unexpected force
Somewhere else. We are all on a great ship
That's lost its balance, lost its way,
And a huge storm's gathering beyond
The iron veil of our hearts. Maybe
It's a storm of revelation. Maybe it's a storm
Of truth, of which art's the unknown magus.
The age is changing. The present moment

Is itself constantly revealing. Everything
We see is the mask of time
Concealing its features.
Come with me through the mask,
Into rites of vision and truth.
Come with me to the blue garden.
New time is being made here from
The wandering sleep of dreamers.
Shadows on the cave walls walk to and fro.
Shadows on the city walls come and go.
Shadows in the garden
Shadows in the garden.
Shadows in the
Shadows.

SLEPT BADLY

a love poem

slept badly.
worked all morning.
i love the view from your window:
jewels scattered in the night.
i want to see the view from your heart.

magic connections will abound.
high force set in motion.
in spite of what you think.
high force set in motion,
connecting above and below.
above in the unseen.
below in the unknown.

i drift in and out of your essence.
reading the runes of your soul.
different inside from outside.
learning a new language
of your faraway breathing.

destiny changes with those secret lines
running through all the webs
far beyond the sphere of time.
there the ones who see beyond
our realm see when the true

genesis of touch bears
astounding fruit.

o how to be ready.
when the dove hovers over
unwilling mind
must you yield up the millennial
ideas of sacrifice.

they know there's no
sacrifice where there's love.
just a giving and an altar-offering
without a name, without
measure. who can measure
the view from your heart?

i sit at its window
and the enigma
of the wild twilight city
makes sense to me
as the movement of the wind
does over the face of the sea.

watch the links multiply,
till a flower is formed.
can you birth a flower?

can you give birth
to the new self that's forming
from the enigma,
a clear form mysterious
to behold, beautiful
as the dawn
over those blue mountains?

what is magic?
touching, and giving birth to worlds.
dreaming, and for the real to be in doubt.
loving, and being calm,
so that all becomes clear
like an angel's evanescent form.

slept badly.
worked all morning.
all i have is a certain gaze of yours.
and the way when leaving
you take all of you with you.
and me at the window,
dreaming.

i want to see the view
from your heart.

LIBERTY

those wings with which
we soar beyond
the mesh of time;
light that blazes
through the darkened
realm of power;
that impulse to tear down
shackles of the soul
bolted there to make us
bend to fear and control.
prometheus's first cry
and his enduring gift.
meaning of myth
when decoded
as fire and light.
prima materia that changes
black earth of suffering
into the red dragon
of bold overcoming.
last flame of a defeated
people, first rekindler
of their resurrection;
yellow path up
to the crowned mountain,
where destiny, mind-forged,
becomes the green ladder

to the lanterned heavens.
secret song of flowers,
and beauty's torch.
my father's injunction,
and my mother's revelation.

A SHAKESPEARE PORTRAIT

You whose mind awakens
Endless generations
Why is your true face so unknown,
And unknowable?
As if you wished to conceal
Your form that you may reveal
That which flows from your soul
To ours, through the inconstancy
Of words, which bring forth
From changing times
Immortal truths, so that justice,
In secret, may prevail.
A balancing hand runs
Through civilisations.
Something mysterious
Ebbs and flows in the sea
Of lives. You show the grace
Of the sea in your hidden face;
But with your dreams
We all stand as one dreamer
In the tempest and the dust.
To know your work
Is not to guess your face;
To see your face is not
To imagine your work.

Your work is a world,
Your face a mask
Behind which the unknown
Master smiles.

NOTRE-DAME IS TELLING US SOMETHING

Notre-Dame's telling us something.
How the orioles weep.
Something in our soul is burning.
Those alchemical flames the flesh
Of our mother is devouring.
Turbulence in the streets;
Rotating anger in the air.
Division across the waters;
Swans of peace live in fear.
Above, the earth dwindles
As mercury consumes the teeth
Of the young and chemicals
Plough the guts of children
Before seeds of death are planted.
No prayers anywhere.
Angels fall like tears;
Winding stairs lead nowhere.
And in Europe the bells are ringing
A dark angelus for faith gone
Underground. A dark mass of unbelief
Stalks the stables and the high tables.
Notre-Dame's telling us something
About the wisdom beyond grief.
We fight over cabbages while
Our spirit perishes in open view.

In alchemy it's when things burn
That they're made true and new.
Orioles are weeping
For the dwindling of our souls
And the smallness of the goals
That obscure cathedrals
And good laws and progress
We've made from wars
To civil liberties, from the comfort
Of our parish minds to the generosity
Of our linked hands.
O the orioles are weeping
For the wars that will be fought
Because of the simple things not taught
Like the underlying unity
And our fundamental trinity
And how when the way is lost
Good things perish
And we will never know the cost.

But Notre-Dame is telling us something
In its flames and its fallen spire.
We've been sinking lower,
Been mesmerised by lies,
Destroying truth,
Instead of rising higher.

Everything that wrenches our hearts
Like signs written in the sky
With invisible hands
Is an inscription to our times
We should read with wise eyes.

Our souls are parched,
Our hearts grow cold.
The young are climate-crisis fighting
Or are in quiet despair perishing
While on the island empire-nostalgia
Secretly and not so secretly obsesses the old.
Our politics keep looking back
To something that never was or has gone
Rather than facing the present
Like the dawn's nightingale song
Or the dew we all lack.
Notre-Dame is saying something
About the holes into which we're falling
Seeking power seeking power
Losing meaning falling tower.
The spire touching the sky
Inclined our eyes up high,
Led us upward to our best selves.
Maybe in these fallen times
While dim bells across Europe chime

That broken spire will re-unite our hearts
Beyond the greed of our diverging ways
Back to pilgrim roads, singing days.
They are singing Ave Marias
Outside flaming Notre-Dame.
And across the world we perhaps
Remember how fine we can be
In the symphony of our deeds
And the harmony of our needs.
For whether it be the Buddhas
Of Bamiyan or Grenfell's grey cladding
Or that home of alchemy and grace
In Paris burning, it's us who burn too,
And the loss is the unborn child's,
The beggar in Timbuktu.
All culture's shared
Beneath the realm
Of sleep and of awakening.
Notre Dame is thundering something.
Awake, O man, awake.
Awake, woman, awake.
The flames are spreading in our sleep.
Flames of the earth.
Flames of future.
Sky-flames
Arctic-flames.

Truth-flames.
Orioles are weeping.
Bells are ringing.
Why are you still sleeping?

A NEW DREAM OF POLITICS

They say there is only one way for politics:
That it looks with cold eyes at the hard world
And shapes it with a ruler's edge,
Measuring what is possible against
Acclaim, support, and votes.

They say there is only one way to dream
For the people, to give them not what they need
But food for their fears.
We measure the deeds of politicians
By their time in power.

But in wiser times they had another way.
They measured greatness by the gold
Of contentment, by the enduring arts,
The laughter at the hearths,
The length of silence when the bards
Tell of what was done by those who
Had the courage to make their lands
Happy, away from war, spreading justice,
Fostering health,
The most precious of the arts
Of governance.

But we live in times that have lost
This tough art of dreaming

The best for the people,
Or so we are told by cynics
And doomsayers who see the end
Of time in blood-red moons.

Always when it is least expected
An unexpected figure
Rises when dreams here have
Become like ash. But when the light
Is woken in our hearts after the long
Sleep, they wonder if it's a fable.

Can we still seek the lost angels
Of our better natures?
Can we still wish and will
For poverty's death and a newer way
To undo war, and find peace in the labyrinth
Of the Middle East, create prosperity
In Africa, and reverse climate change
As true ways to end fear
And the feared tide of immigration
And bring greater harmony to our world?

We are dreaming a new politics
That will renew the world
Under their weary and suspicious gaze.

There's always a new way,
A better way that's not been tried before.
A way that becomes a fable.

CLOSED, STILL OPEN

For Anda Winters

how do we improvise in these difficult times?
how to keep our art and spirit alive?
we have to find a new way into the future
that is better than the way of the past.
perhaps now like children who have
woken the kraken from the deep
we'll learn which laws
of life to keep.

no more can we blame god
or the gods. we are the evil
that keeps on coming back to us.
it's time to re-examine our histories.
find a new road to the future.
get back to the balance we've lost
or we are on the path to dust.
our past has led us here.
but to have a radiant future
a new consciousness is needed.
something brave, beyond fear.
this must be the time of awakening.
the kraken's here.

can we in these times improvise?
upwards our dreams must we revise.

THE UNKNOWN HOUR

It is often the question in life
Whether to stay or leave.
It's a fundamental thing we believe.
History began with staying or leaving.
We stayed in the garden long
Enough for celestial history
To ripen, the slow completion
Of that cosmic task. There was no time
In the garden. Neither clocks, nor necessity,
Nor referendums presided over
Our ancestors' temporal stay.
There was no need to leave;
Only a deed obscured behind a deed
Forced the angel to send us out.
History, some say, is the secret
Effort to get back there.
Some say there would be no
Evolution without being cast out.
But being thrown out is different
To leaving. For leaving is a voluntary
Act. A severing. Disowning. A cutting off.
No one who knew the war, misery,
Untold and untellable suffering
Of life outside the garden would have left
Voluntarily. This is of course a metaphor.
Not to be taken on a razor's edge.

To want to leave Europe is not the same
As leaving Eden. For Eden was perfection,
And nothing afterwards can ever be. Only
Degrees of imperfection, degrees of beauty,
Degrees of agreeable possibility, scope for
Growth and mutual growth, the space in which
To help one another on the difficult journey
Back to the rose garden, is maybe the best
That we can hope for. Those who sell some thing
As the perfect dream always sell a lie.

2

I think we grow best through mutuality.
The world grows more complex. Outside
The windows of our nations, great forces
Swell and array their ranks in finance and in arms.
As they grow bigger, we grow smaller.
It was the unwise fate of African nations
To huddle vulnerably under isolated
Flags. Easily picked off by the plunging eagles.
Easy prey. Justice on this earth demands
A new balance of forces against the secret
Armies gathering in the night. Weapons
Of evil shuttle across borders in the dark.
Terrorism has become the ordinary language
Of our broken speech, the shout of those who
Want to compel others to bow to their book or creed.

3

An invisible line connects us all and everything
Is now linked in tears and pain. No longer
Is there a place in which we can hide our head
From the bombs and the curses and the violence
That is the air of our times. A problem here scuttles
Across seas and borders and no high walls or policed
Boundaries can return the prestige of nations
To innocence ever again. We have entered
The age of migrations, mass migrations,
Of breaking across borders and of wars that send
Whole populations shifting the fragile
Geography of the globe into something
  unrecognisable.
The vengeance of the lost garden is ours at last.
There's no other way than back to what
The garden meant, which we have forgotten.
The garden wasn't many. It was always one.
Now we are millions. Our ways are legion;
Our dreams fragmented. The garden was one.
Only in the return to the one can there be
Any peace in the fury of history. Broken
And divided we're all doomed and merely
Awaiting the unknown forms of destruction
Which time and the grim consequences
Of our deeds and dreams will perfect.
Everywhere nations breaking away from larger

Nations. Fragmentation. Fragmentation.
Is there a future in fragmentation upon
    fragmentation?
Perhaps those who remain together as one, uniting
Their diverse gifts, making beauty out of chaos,
Begin to reverse the entropic trend of life
Beyond the first garden. To fall is not to fall
From space or height. It is to fall from unity,
From oneness. But it's easier to walk out
Than to work it out. Easier to fall apart
Than to stay together. The romance of independence,
Of freedom, seems stronger than the truth of unity.
That's why it took no time to fall
And all of history and future history
To return. Sometimes one thing speaks
For another. Its resonance sounds a warning bell.

4

It seems wars are about separation
Not unity. The compulsion
Of force, the forced unity, is not unity
But an improbable army whose designs
We recognise in the canon fire,
The drones and the nuclear threat.
But what the toxic air whispers
In the children's poisoned milk,

What the clouds know and the seas mutter
And the mercury-laden fish threaten
And the murders in the name of religion
Or in the perversion of the many names of God
Or the cyclical battles of the eagle and the snake
Or the hyper growth of poverty
While the multinationals and corporations
Rule subterranean realities
Of land and sea and sky, calls us to a choice.

5

Ah, but the wisdom of neti neti.
Neither this nor that, neither that nor this.
Ancient Greece believed we must choose.
But you touch one end of the scale
And in time it swings to the other side.
Peace swings to war,
War swings to peace.
Ah but the wisdom of neti neti.
Which of our choices are absolute in the good
They bring? How often has good brought
Evil through an unknown door, how often
Has evil brought good from a secret path?
Some shout for an independence never lost.
Others sing for a union never truly found.
One shout, and a gun is fired;

A knife is stabbed into the flesh.
Who knows the destiny of our insistence?
Sometimes it takes an innocent
Death to wake the confused conscience
Of a nation. Sometimes it takes a bad decision
To make clear the truth that wasn't seen
In the screen of our contingent quarrels and fears
Awoken by demagogues with secret
Ambitions. We never really appreciate
The transforming effects of our good decisions.
Our inspired ignorance.

6

Sometimes it's best not to choose but to wait.
Often we hurry to choose before we know what
We are choosing. Lost is the wisdom of waiting.
Neti neti. Neither this nor that. Neither that nor this.
Waiting the way destiny does, the way trees do,
Spending all winter and spring to decide about
    summer.
Meanwhile all that's true within them always
Growing, lifting the antinomy of life and of death.
They grow when they can, they die when they can't.
Given half a chance they always grow back,
On concrete or stone or the side of a hill.

It seems to me this is a great law: be
Impenetrable to death, tenacious of life,
Open to its subtleties, paradoxes, and not
Incapacitated by the complex dance of stone and sea,
Rock and wind, sunlight and cloud, night and stars.
It is never clear what things really are till long
After the ashes have nourished the pear
The apple, the rose and the vine.

7

And long after, when the planter cannot remember
What was planted, whether it was crocodile or stone,
A blood-red flag, a nuclear fist, a blue flower
As big as the sea, a fear-fruit vast
As a yellow mountain, or even a stream
That wanders over hidden lodes of gold and myths,
Long after, when the tares and the wheat
Are mingled in forgotten fires,
An inevitable fate, whose mathematics
We cannot disentangle, will stand inside us,
A half-begotten tree of darkness and of hope
That we might not recognise as our own,
In the garden we didn't harvest
In the garden in which we did not invest
In a time which is in a momentary arrest,
Frozen between the before and after,

When the before was not what we thought
And the after is not what we know,
As time mixes intentions and outcomes
The way the earth mixes the dead
And the living into enigma harvests.
What did we plant, what does time reap?
Between the planting and reaping
A world of karmic fruitions,
Future necessities, the unspeakable progeny
Of the past. Time doesn't reap what we sow,
But something altogether more strange.
Do not speak to me about the direct relation
Between past and present, or present and future.
Life yields what we never expect.
Each moment of our being deserves respect.

8

Consequences attend our secret deeds
And our public acts like figures taking form
In a dream. Only the dream is real.
The world is the dream we've made.
That's why history and history's fruits
Are so unreal. So unreal are the fruits
Our lives eat. Unreal before and after.
Ongoing unreality in the reality of time.
Each day's events like dreams in a billboard.

Sunflower nightmares. Creeping vines of fear.
The maternal earth absorbing storm and sunlight.
But shaken by whether we stay or leave.
The earth too feels our staying or leaving
Like flowers do, or pictures on a wall
When the dead return and find
That no one's home. Only the wind
Rattling windowpanes of history.
Or they return and find that we've
Forgotten them, and they resume
Their old habits in our living spaces
While the fingers of evening climb
High on the white walls, and the clock
Strikes an hour no one knows.

Convergence

LINES ON A DRAWING

For Rosemary Clunie

they found a way
through four
dimensions of the door
to raise my play.

this is the game
where love's the name

for every music heard
there are tears unheard

when one can't sing
when one can't sing
there is a bird
that dies
as it flies

love these drawings
of our tender evenings

every line
is a note
from the heart
to the divine

be joyful,
spartacus.

OUTSIDE THE WEDDING

the pen moves with
the power of eros;
but the graves hold
back my desire.
it's hard for dreams to rise
above the speech
and yet transcend the fire.
graves make me think
of how our loves and hopes
with time and weight do sink.
and yet eros rises higher.
outside the wedding feast
the road runs past
the field of fine roses
and stone crosses
and black birds on
the black telegraph wire.
then the graves make me drink.
they stop the gaze.
it can go no further.
but the pen moves
to the power of eros,
and eros just rises higher.

EVEREST

some visions draw
us to impossible places.
visions that live
in the heart
of our mythologies.
they pull us like ants, up
into white clouds
at the edge of dream.
how many have perished
in the storm or snow?
their tracks vanished.
whiteness obliterates
the centuries.
but some visions
demand only
snow-eaten feet,
ice-broken hands.
that white stony
visage disdains history.
into the abyss of its mouth
pale generations go
like sleepwalkers.
sometimes a single storm
blots out our elaborate plans.

civilisation climbs its face
and with a breath is erased again.
all dreams lead here.
from this lunar elevation
everything seems clear:
we must either sit still
or overcome ourselves.
we're the mountains
we need to climb;
we're our own impossible peak.
everything that we seek
is dissolved by success;
only the trackless path
is worth travelling on.
some dreams do draw us up,
not towards any particular eminence,
but to something of which
this mountain is but a mysterious
symbol, whose meaning eludes us
and ever drives us on, drives us
up, with the blinding sun in our eyes.

it holds up a mirror
to our fevers, our delirium,
our hopes and our need to conquer.
and there we are shattered

there we are made.
it is one of the forms
of the divine, perplexing
the riddle of distance.
is it a call to heroism
or a dream of oblivion?
everyone who ascends
descends into a polar space,
where the far is near
and the near farther
than valhalla.

some visions draw us to
impossible places
where breathing's a new
language in the wind
where we can climb
higher into the flame of the days
the flowering of the streets
the dim ritual of work
the initiation of sleep
and the clarity of home.

because one person did something
vaguely unthinkable,
perhaps impossible,

because one person did,
others can till their fields
or leap to the moon
dance in a ring of fire
or walk treadmill incarnations
towards the centre of that vast
invisible red rose.

                    *

you who climb up
and you who sit beneath a tree
and you who at your desk
await a vision, perhaps an annunciation
you who scratch at your thoughts
till your life bleeds
you frozen in fear, or blistered in rage
singing on a vacant stage
you in poverty or in wealth
some vision draws us on
which we must heed
or not be born.

HAMLET

we're always asking ourselves
why this young man is so intense.
there's something about him
that's more than what he seems.
the play ends and you have a sense
of something unfinished.
as if it were a step
in an obscure initiation.
how confined that world seems,
as if elsinore were an alchemical
vessel where all the heat
of those passions served only
to transform the inner temperature
of some subterranean event.
but he's not what he is.
the world he's enclosed in
is only part of a long journey.
part of an ongoing process.
do you know the next stage?
it might be written in a hundred years;
perhaps it's been composed
already: a novel, a poem,
a painting whose meaning
always eludes us till
we approach the figure
at the threshold.

can't escape the feeling
of the unfinished.
that death ends nothing. why?
nothing is diminished.
because another death
is referred to, not the death
of one person, with a name
and a history, but another death,
we must pass through
on the way to a mysterious
light. but how like a phase
in the great work it feels,
not calcination, with its black
earth and its skull,
but something further down
the liminal process,
like fermentation, where a deep
change has begun, the intellect
awoken, the soul coming out
of its coarse material shell,
to glimpse the infinite heavens

A LITTLE SONG

the sun's smiling at me today
even when the snow's here.
birds are full of wonder
at the changing celestial sphere

my heart's warm with laughter
the roads are clear
girls are walking on frost
with the lights in their hair

the sky's an undreamed-of palette
and branches are sifting the wind
all things are secretly dreaming
of passion and mysterious spring

February 1991

IN A TEMPLE IN SEOUL

is it penance or an act
in a long journey
to true enlightenment?
sacrifice or a rite
of purification,
symbolic rite,
spiritual discipline,
lesson or the koan
of a noviciate?

in the temple these
questions haunt me
as i contemplate
the woman who
polishes the wooden
floor till it shines
like the buddha's light.

without a pause,
and with thoroughness,
she polishes and cleans
places that are already
polished and clean,
with her cloth mop.

whatever we tread on
she cleans.
her act is perpetual.
the purpose isn't
merely to shine the floor,
nor merely to get rid
of dirt. her purpose seems
more mysterious,
as though she wants
to eliminate the minutest speck
of dust and dirt
from the calm presence
of the gold buddha.

the temple is a beautiful
riot of colours: greens,
yellows, and reds.
dragons loom with tongues
of fire from high places.
yet, for all that colour,
such calm.

the space there is vaster
than it seems
and peace adds dimensions
to a room, a study or temple.

we sit on prayer mats,
cross-legged, surrounded
by one thousand
buddhas. a small kama
for carrying women
in ancient times
rests in a blue corner.
the decorated drum
on a stand
resonates in silence.

all around us
the woman polishes
every inch of the floor.
works without emotion.
cleansing
the universe
of suffering
and sin.

CONVERGENCE

For Michael Aminian

language from the mouths.
screams from the earth.
all around the globe is burning.
deep inside we're all connected.
world is bleeding,
soul is reeling,
there's a global fever
and money is weeping
only the poor shed tears
above the earth.
sustenance is dwindling.
clouds glow with poisoned fumes.
we think we're safe
but we're breathing in death,
the death of dreams
and all that it means.
oil spews ruining farmlands.
innocent shores receive
the west's toxic waste
palmtree forests
have become rivers of oil slick;
mountains of gold
have become craters of dead stones.
have you seen the mountain
wastes of tanzania where

they mine the earth
and fill it with dark fear?
have you gone deep
into the grim bowels
of mozambique
and been buried for less
than an apple's price?
there's a weird logic in the world.
the truly rich countries are poor
and the truly poor countries are rich.
where there should be
harvests of ripe laughter
there are just the shadows
of hungry children in the streets.
there's a red dust
in the blue skies of guinea;
the bauxite pulled from its earth
like golden teeth
could sprinkle paradise
from the red soil.
but the earth is burned
and mango trees lean out
from open mines.
many lands with their shacks
and abundant trashheaps,
orange umbrellas in marketplaces

and gas combustion on the edge
of forests have an infernal doorway
into ever-vanishing paradise.
in marikana the spirits of apartheid
endure in crooked ventures.

dance with me along the timeline.
the silk road and the spice trade route
have thrown out red bridges
to little villages
with tents and shimmering deserts.
the real history of the future will be
the story of the transformation of the poor;
· from kolkata to lagos,
from london to laos,
from nuremberg to timbuktu.
There's a new language on the lips:
either justice or death,
either collaboration
or the fire of the gods
hurled by the unforgiving hunger
of the world's broken children.
it's time to change the nature of the game,
time to write on the face of the earth
the value and meaning of every name.

OBAMA

Sometimes the world is changed
When the right person appears.
But the right person
Is also the right time.
The time and the person
Have to work the secret
Alchemy together.

To change the world is more
Than just changing its laws.
Sometimes it's just
Being a new possibility,
A portal through which new
Fire can enter this world
Of folly and error.

They change the world best who
Alter the way we think.
For our thoughts make our world.
Some think it's our deeds;
But deeds are the visible
Children of thought.
The thought-changers are the game-
Changers, are the life-changers.
We think achievements are symbols.
But symbols aren't symbols.

They are often what they
Are in themselves.
Obama is not a mere symbol.
Sometimes even a symbol is a sign
That we aren't dreaming potently
Enough. A sign that the world is the home
Of possibility. A sign that our chains
Are unreal. That we're freer than we
Know, that we're more powerful than
We dare to think. If he's a symbol,
Then it's of some kind of liberation.
A symbol also that power in this world
Can't do everything. Even Moses couldn't
Set his people free. They had to
Wander in the wilderness. They too
Turned against their leaders
And away from their God
And had to overcome themselves
And their history to arrive
At the vision their prophets
Had long before.
Being a Black president
Is not a magic wand
That will make all
Black problems disappear.
Leaders alone cannot

Undo all the evils that
Structural evil makes
Natural in the life
Of a people. Not just leadership;
Structures must change.
Structures of thought
Structures of dreams
Structures of injustice
Structures that keep
A people imprisoned
To the stones and the dust
And the ash and the dirt,
The dry earth, the dead roads.

Always we look to our leaders
To change what we ourselves must change
With the force of our voices and the force
Of our souls and the strength of our dreams
And the clarity of our visions and the strong
Work of our hands. Too often we get fixated
On symbols. We think fame ought to promote
Our cause, that presidents ought to change our
Destinies, that more of our faces on television
Will somehow make life easier and more just
For our people. But symbols ought to only be
A sign to us that the power is in our hands.

Mandela ought to be a sign to us that we cannot
Be kept down, that we are self-liberating.
And Obama ought to be a sign to us that
There's no destiny in colour. There is only
Destiny in our will and our dreams and the storms
Our *nos* can unleash and the wonder our *yesses*
Can create. But we have to do the work ourselves
To change the structures so we can be free.
Freedom is not colour; freedom is thought

An attitude, a power of spirit,
A constant self-definition.
So what Obama did and did
Not do is neither here nor there,
In the great measure of things.
History knows what he did, against the odds.
History knows what he could not do.
Not that his hands were tied,
But that those who resent
The liberation of one who
Ought not to be liberated
Blocked those doors and those roads
And whipped up those sleeping
And those not so sleeping demons
Of race, twin deities of America.
And they turned his *yes* into *no*

Just so they could say that they told us so,
Told us that colour makes ineffectuality,
Colour makes destiny.
They wanted him to fail so they
Could prove their case.
Can't you see it?
But that's what heroes do:
They come right through
All that blockage,
All those obstacles thrown
In the path of the self-liberated.
Then the symbol would be tainted
And would fail to be a beacon
And a sign that it is possible
To be black and great.
Ali overcame that tough fate.
Mandela transfigured white hate.
Obama, twice, became the head of state.

I don't trust mirrors. Many of them lie.
We need dreams to show us what we can be
And images to show us where we are.
What we are is too nebulous to be defined
By class or colour or gender or height.
We are beyond definition. The state
Can't measure our true estate.

Not the school we attended
Nor our parent's name, nor the university
We studied at, nor the forms of apprenticeship
That life offered can define or measure
Our cosmic potentiality.
No one can define us except ourselves.
From the beginning of time no such
Limit was ever made as part
Of the immortal truth of things.
No god, no race,
No force, no state,
No secret prejudice
Can set a seal
On what we are,
What we can be.
For we are made
With the first force
That shaped the stars
And galaxies.
That's all I want to say.
Changers of the world
Say it in their own way.

Midday

AFRICA IS A REALITY NOT SEEN

africa is a reality not seen
a dream not understood
its wars are the scab of a wound
its famine the cracking of seeds
its dictatorships a child torturing
beetles in a field.

its soul's older than atlantis
and like all things old,
it's being reborn,
and doesn't know it.

countless cycles of civilisation
and destruction are lost in its memory
but not in its myths.

africa is a living enigma
an old woman taken for a child
a wise man taken for a fool
a beggar who is also a great king.

A BROKEN SONG

For Ken Saro-Wiwa

that he was jailed
and tortured
and killed
for loving his homeland
the earth
and crying out at its
defilement is
monstrously unfitting
we live in unnatural times
and we must make
them natural again
with our wailing

for unnatural times
then become natural
by tradition
and by silence.
that is why the nations
today ring out
with injustice
with lies
with prejudice
made natural

the earth deserves our love
only the unnatural ones
can live at ease
while they poison the lands
rape her for gain
bleed her for oil
and not even attempt
to heal her wounds

only unnaturals
rule our nations today
so deaf to the wailing
of our skies, of the hungry
of the strange new diseases
and of that dying earth
bleeding, wounded,
and breeding grim deserts
where once there were
proud trees of africa
cleaning their rich green hair
in the bright winds of heaven

that he was jailed
for loving his homeland
and tortured
and killed

for protecting his own people
and crying out
like the ancient town criers did
at the defilement of the earth
is monstrously unfitting.
we live in an unnatural age
and we must make
it natural again
with our singing
our intelligent rage

DECOLONISATION

From Fanon

it never takes place unnoticed.
like a blade before your eyes.
it transforms those crushed with
their nothingness into central
performers under the floodlight
of history's blood-like gaze.
a new rhythm, by dew
men brought, a language new
minted from the old
earth, a humanity remade
by vaporising chains
and the brutal alembic
of oppression. it's the way
new beings are forged,
from fire and rage,
distilled into clear dawn.
but nothing supernatural
presides over this renewal.
no deities or heroes
or famed individuals.
the new becomes
being the same way
it became free.

ON RACE

ignorance thinks there's black and white
ignorance thinks there's them and us
ignorance thinks of outsiders and insiders
ignorance thinks about skin and not heart
ignorance thinks one race is better than another
ignorance thinks people should be kept apart
ignorance thinks nothing unites us all
ignorance fears the foreign and unknown
ignorance is the soul of cowardice and fear
ignorance speaks and darkness forms in the air
ignorance will destroy this world with hate
wisdom with light will change that fate

THE INSIDER

After Camus

I wasn't laughing.
I should have laughed.
Maybe if I'd laughed everything
Would have been different.
So it wasn't me laughing.
It was the sun.
The sun was laughing through
The stones, the sand,
The sluggish sea.

He did not even know my name.
He did not know the name of my sister.
This is my country and to them
I do not have a name.

I do not even have a face.
How can you be sure I exist?
But this land is my land
And I have a right to be here.
I can be here, lie here
And listen to the sun
Steaming the sand.

My life's a flute
Played by the sun.

And because of the sun
I've a right to honour.
I have not one
Name, but thousands;
And my names are written
By the waves of the sea
On the hot earth.

Each rock's a punctuation.
The words of the Prophet
Are the secret truth of my days.
I am my own meaning.
All the names of the land
Are my names and even
In the shadow of this rock
I am nourished
By the love of mothers.

I watch him coming towards me.
His heart's unclear.
For him there's no meaning
To anything; the universe
Is empty and life is a road
That wanders into nothingness.
The sun that gives me life
Lacerates him with death.

It's not that we are enemies.
It's only that for him
Everything means nothing
But for me life has dignity.
Life has meaning.
Maybe that's why
It is easy for them
To kill with their
Eyes that which to
Them has no name.

If we could talk I might
Tell him my name's
Mamoud and that
Two weeks ago
My mother died
And I am all
My sister has
To protect her against
The violence of the world.

But I am not laughing.
Life's grimace looks
Like laughter to one who
Wants to see it that way.

MANETHO'S BOOKS

when they come to the source
they always want information.
when they conquer they want
the secrets of the land
that its priests conceal.
and so the incas would rather
let the spaniards have the gold
which for them had little value
than reveal to them their temples
or the heart of their tiered gnosis
or their gods high up
the mountains where
peak speaks to peak
among the clouds,
the rockfaces terraced
and textured for agriculture.

ptolemy wanted the secrets
of the land of pyramids
and ordered the high priest
at sebennytus, where isis
has her temple, to write down
the dreams, philosophy
the narrative and religion
of ancient egypt. we don't know
if manetho asked why.

we don't know either what
manetho concealed in what he
revealed in the innumerable
volumes that flowed
from his hermes-touched stylus.
but ptolemy forbade their translation
and they were used only
for the solemn instruction
of the greeks.

manetho's books were the central
columns of alexandria.
students of aristotle drank
from his fountain. egyptian
priests were professors at
the alexendrine schools.
eratosthenes composed,
under the impulse of the greek
spear, a chronology
of theban kings. horapollo
wrote the purest hieroglyphics
of his time. the true story
of civilisation is more obscure
than the oracles and more
twisted than cyrenean snakes.

SIWAH

sometimes journeys defy explanation.
rather, the branching off from a journey
confuses the intimate and public history.
a child plays in the hills; something
makes them wander through runnels where
they find clay pots, old assyrian shards,
or the cave of lascaux. no one knows
what made them do it, or what they
were seeking blindly in the diversion
from play, the journey made
from the back of another one.
the unplanned surprises
the fates weave as they spin
the future of all pasts. a glitch
appears in their spinning,
a bubble in the weave, an abrasion
of colours, which only art can correct.
we call that art destiny surprising us back
in echo response to our unplanned deeds.

take that famous visit to the oracle
of ammon. he'd already exhausted
himself with wars and the vast desert.
he had already pursued the edges
of personal destiny as far as it could go,
extending the limits. But the sands

were writhing with pitiless snakes
and the troops were already famished
with this conquest without
end, till the world runs out.
the persians had been routed; there
was nothing more to win except
rest and the spoils of hard conquest.
but obscure urges dwell in the hearts
of those who toil at world domination.
some say he was perplexed
by the mystery of his origins,
that he sought a father more
elevated than the mortal one,
that baffled by the teeming myths
that sprang up in his body, giving him
no rest, driving him on through numberless
obstacles, that he sought to understand
whether divinity played a part in the strange
shapes that the fates wove in his dreams,
and whispered in his long marches,
his encounters with wandering sages
and pointed through him to the sun.

he abandoned his troops and took
with him few men, and risked death
by thirst and black snakes through

that harsh desert where myths
are ruined or forged. history
relates, with more fact than truth,
that he stationed a garrison at pelusium
and along the eastern nile to heliopolis
traversed the river to memphis.
he'd struck through the burnished desert.
at memphis they crowned him pharoah.
apis received his sacrificial bulls
and the canonic branch of the nile
witnessed his branching off journey
to the fertile oasis in siwah. his greek
sandals trod as far as paraetonium,
in ancient libyia, leaving small footprints
like dead fishes on those salt shores
of dead rivers. what did he seek
in that hallucination, that obscure quest
to the heart of myth? he disappeared
into the temple and only silence
and an unknowable man emerged
from between its tall gates.
not the same man came out as went in
some spoke of a new light on his face.
some spoke of a serenity in his eyes
that had never been there before.
the priests of that temple, where

philosophers came to be raised,
had whispered something magical
into his ears which he hadn't heard
and in not hearing heard everything
he had ever wanted and sought
in all the disguised battles of his life.
more than all the things we're told,
the finger pointing to the sun
in him, touched another gold.

BOKO HARAM

an unfinished poem

he came from a house
where light hadn't been,
a hole of poverty
in the depths of the north.
the ghetto where he grew
brought him madness.
at school he kept
apart and was silent.
his eyes stared with fury.
early on he dressed
in clothes of the fanatics.
his religion came with the gun
and the loathing of beauty.
he nibbled the koran
with dreams of death.
he watched politicians
grow fat while his mother
rotted in the vile hovels
where dogs ate the corpses
of those who had died poor
and unknown. the fervid
sun ruined his mind.
he joined a sect and prayed
with a jihadi's gun
always by his side.

when the leader
of his sect was killed
he disappeared.
no one saw him for years.
in his absence girls grew up
and dreamed of school.
the ghettoes were rotting.
schools were spreading.
girls learned to read
and count and think
and dream and soon
measure the lies.
when he returned he'd
changed out of all form.
took to murder,
blowing up streets
where the christians lived.
he grew bold. ammunitions
came to him from secret
places. again the north
held the nation's fate,
born from a distant dream.
in the tall grass girls
chanted their songs
in the long shadows.

AMNESTY AT FORTY

The Lesson

Tyranny rises where vigilance sleeps
The light of freedom makes us strong
Tyranny rises where vigilance sleeps
The light of freedom makes us strong
Tyranny rises where vigilance sleeps
The flight of freedom makes us wrong
Tyranny rises where vigilance sleeps
The light of freedom makes us strong
Tyranny rises where vigilance sleeps
The light of freedom makes us strong
Tyranny rises where vigilance sleeps
The light of freedom makes us strong
Tyranny rises where freedom sleeps
The light of vigilance makes us strong
Tyranny rises where vigilance sleeps
The light of freedom makes us strong
Tyranny rises where vigilance sleeps
The light of freedom makes us strong
Tyranny rises where freedom sleeps
The light of freedom makes us strong
Tyranny rises where vigilance sleeps
The light of reason makes us strong
Tyranny rises where   sleeps
The light of freedom makes us strong

Tyranny rises where vigilance sleeps
The light of freedom makes us strong
Tyranny rises where vigilance sleeps
The light of freedom makes us strong
Tyranny rises where vigilance sleeps
The light of freedom makes us strong
Tyranny sleeps where vigilance rises
The light of freedom makes us strong
Tyranny rises where vigilance sleeps
The light of freedom makes us strong
Tyranny rises where vigilance sleeps
The light of freedom makes us strong
Tyranny rises where vigilance sleeps
The light of reason makes us strong
Tyranny rises where vigilance sleeps
The light of freedom wakes us

REVOLUTION

they live as if everything
is settled in the world.
but nothing is settled.
not our dreams, nor our fears,
nor the boundary between things.
the land isn't settled, nor the realm of sleep.
nor the deep mines where our fathers weep.
nor the deep wells where
mothers call out our names.
those walls of steel never kept out
the eyes of hunger that wander the world
like thunder. those stony eyes that devour
the poor with a cold gaze,
those tower blocks, those men who live
on dust and sleep on stones,
those mothers with their teeth
falling out from mercury in their food,
those children whose lungs will
not carry them through life
what do they know of boundaries,
what do they know of the gods
of the street, the gods of hunger.

nothing is settled. not our place
in the world nor our place among the dead.
the rich have not locked up all the dreams

or the power that grows in rage.
generations live on dust and debris
and are pale as ghosts but the god
of hunger powers their bodies with the secret
electricity that drives galaxies.
on the city's edge they swell and grow.
their only education is the text of truth
which the world delivers without humour.

nothing is settled. those who think they will
inherit the earth because they've mortgaged
the sun will find on the eve of their usurpation
that the grim horsemen are on the horizon.
the earth shifts and howls. the sands have
turned into people. the graves speak
lucid prophecies. there's nothing
to inherit, because nothing is settled,
except the thunder after sleep.

Dusk

A HISTORY OF NEW FORMS

For David Hammons

hairy stone
on white stool
on metal stand.
brooding about
lost air,
incandescent paint.

those tarpaulin
concealments.
mirrors dripping
dark celestial matter.
the fan in which
wind is still.

yellow table
where caravaggio
is beheaded.
old testament
of duchamp
made into
the history
of harlem.
beyond masks
floating on sea
new dream

breaks through
hands
of silent
enchanter.

here's where
new african
genius is made,
changing the dream-
less lids
of duchamp
into the spring
of hammons.

blue time passing.
smaller
form,
bigger
conversation.

keep moving
it away
from what
it was.
from old
field,
new time.

music
in the stone.
alchemy
in the transcended
american air.

art is that book
in which history
of new forms
is written.
by the firedreams
of harlem.

throwing
the stone
into open sea
into sunrise
over brooklyn.

REVELATIONS OF SAINT TIME

For Grace Wales Bonner

everything here is kind of true.
the true magic is the magic of you.
the world's the shrine
and the shrine's the world.
listen here to
the revelations of saint time.
still your hearts. breathe like new.
centre yourselves in the part
of you that's most true.
for every cell of your body
is alive with vitality
every thought in your heart
helps to shape reality.
We're shaping a new reality today
the way you would shape a new shrine
with the offering of your spirit
and the magical works of your hand.
we're going to start a new kind
of dreaming in this land.

awake! awake! awake!

awaken the new brotherhood of dreams
awaken the new sisterhood of dreams.
from these flowers

draw new powers
build new towers.
build without fear.
It's fear that darkens the shrine of the world.
It's greed that darkens the shrine of the heart

stone at your feet
stone in the mind
frozen blood in the veins
dark rock in the heart.
we need a new miracle of being human.
we need a new miracle of being alive.

ancestors sleep in these shrines.
us their dreams illumine.
they planted these flowers
along black paths of time
flowers that never die
flowers that open up into
thousand forms of art and living
music in the flowers
flowers in the music.
so dedicate yourselves
to the shrine
of being and living.

wake up your feet
to the wisdom
of the earth
open your head
to the wisdom
of the heavens
listen to the whispers
breathe the fragrance
of survivors.

windrush, chainrust, slaveburst.
ancestors dreaming in the shrines.
us their courage,
us their fire illumines.
shine a light that's so bright
it burst all the darkness.
write the magic of our souls
on the darkness of the night.
like stars the shrines
stream out the veiled brilliance
of the ancestors
who with the clarity of their thought
opened up new futures.
those triple-locked steel doors
that we open with the magic touch
of our light-charged spirit.

oh but the spirits are singing
in the hidden glow
the more they keep us down
the greater we will grow.

they're rowdy and they know.
they know
they know
they know

they know the revelations of saint time
things that every day are becoming true
coming up through the shrine
coming up for me and for you.

COSMOSIS

For Tony Allen

let us talk about the science
of how things break;
how the heart breaks;
how the age founders and shatters,
with no one listening;
how the mind quakes,
how we lose all that matters.
    oh the music of the bones,
     music of flowers and wise stones

let's talk about the art
of how things break
things that were hard to make
things like peace and love and mead
how the lands shake
how the good is lost to the fake
    oh breathe change by osmosis
     change and the music of cosmosis

but sufis sing of how things turn
things the others want to bury or burn
things like unity, friendship, relativity
things that when dead we'll mourn
how the music runs in the stream
can we in these troubled times dream?
    oh the spirits dancing in the slipstream
     power and fire in the drumdream

MOTHER DANCE

surprise at being a mother.
always had the dream.
always had the fear.
sometimes the life and dream
seem in conflict.
had to stop being
a warrior to go through
that door.
but the spirit of this child
called to me from afar
deep in the fire of dance.
she's the dance, the real dance
of life and love and truth.
in her birth was i born again
into the mysterious world
of motherhood. tuned in,
more than a twin,
to her every cry and need.
the child makes the mother,
and the mother blesses the world.

FOR MIRABELLA

she turned up in the world
with a half-smile on her face.
i've been puzzled by that half-smile.
no one tells you how hard it is.
best if it's kept secret.
it's a kind of initiation
into some of the secret truths
of life. didn't sleep twenty minutes
in eight days. that's nothing compared
to how hard for the mother it has been.
she's been graceful and brave.
the quality of love changes
with this little being who's come
from somewhere else
to expand our lives. time
changes too with the birth.
a child is an absorbent
concentration of time, is time itself.
both as metaphor and living fact.
it's enough to say that
which was promised is now present;
and with her something has
mysteriously changed in the world.
breathing tastes different.
the nature and even the speed
of my dreams have altered.

about the joy itself i cannot speak,
for it defies me all about, being
mixed with many strange numinous
things, all magical, all greater
than the heart can translate.
something to do with realms
beyond, into which my
being has been interpolated,
head stuck in a furnace of the divine.
you expect it to burn,
but instead deep water
hallelujahs sound in
flowers and oracles.
one suddenly wanders
the earth aware that our
little life's fringed
with the miraculous
unnamed, part darkness,
and part splendour.
all this is a way of saying that
i'm humbled and silent.
that half-smile silenced me.
half-smile at the gate of being.
only the rest of your life will
reveal what it means, what it was
you knew as you shot out
into the strange waters of life.

DANCE OF THE NEW BORN

- from warmth
- into the cold
- sprung
- hover
- mother, you?
- shiver
- can't sleep
- can't wake
- where am i?
- who am i?
- where is this?
- twitching
- stretching
- hold me
- feed me
- everything new
- being here
- staying here
- learning to see
- smells
- sounds
- that face, that face!
- helpless
- carried
- gravity
- being… loved

– okay, i'm here
– oh dear, i'm here
– i'm here

BALLET OF THE UNSEEN

For Charlotte Jarvis

ballet of the unseen gathers into itself
unseen suffering and the unseen joys.
the dances unnoticed.

the indigo moods of women.
and the hidden tangents of growth.

lost dreams of street corners;
and the secret angles of trees.

movements lost in the long history of dance.

to celebrate the unseen poetry of movement is
its hope.

the shift and dazzle of marketplaces;

the stillness of the temple where the goddess
whirls;

the politics of the powerless who sing strength
with their taut bodies.

and the electric arabesques of the prayers for
truth…

it helps to have an anchor even if it's symbolic.

dance hangs upon a thread of hope.

all that movement held by a gaze of love.

oh, to start a new dance across the world

choreographed by the spirit of integration

to dream of such liberation
is why i work with gravity and sunlight

and moonwind, and tidelift;
earthturn and relativity.
quantum motions.
notations of spirit.
footleaps and breath.

the way a dancer manages her fall

into gifts of freedom.

to write dance the way one writes poetry.

to write poetry the way one writes dance.

our motion and stillness.

our masks and our faces.

the thoughts you cannot think.
the dreams you cannot dream.
that which only a mask can see.
lost chlorophyll of feet walking across a field.

womb of the tree.
the dancer in meditation
before jagged lines of a twig.
the unseen dance in a dancer's meditation.
the stillness of the mask that pulls a child across a
    field.

seasons in a garden with the trees still.
and the mask dreaming
and the footsteps retreating.
the playground of the world.

all our lives an infinite improvisation.
twirling and being reborn.
dying and then resurrecting
at the foot of the tree.
the single tree that spreads its branches in our souls.
the great world tree.

and the return
and the study
and the starting again
from first position.

SHAVED HEAD POEM

living in testing times.
most testing times in one
hundred years. pandemic
sweeping through our
world will wipe clean
pages of the human story.
nothing will be unchanged
in its wake. strikes at the core
of what it means to be human.
strikes at the heart
of culture and of civilisation.
culture depends on dialogue
and civilisation depends
on communality.

first time in the history
of the human we're compelled
to survive on little
contact with each other.
it's as if the earth, exhausted
with the monstrosities
of our deeds and follies has
pressed the reset button
on humanity by sending
us this nightmare.

for too long now
we've wallowed in excess.
we've wrought damage
on the world in a relentless
pursuit of wealth.
we've taken and taken
exhausted the teats
of mother earth
dried up the wells
of renewal
given ourselves over
to exploitation and to greed.
we're like the children of israel
whom the prophets
found in orgies,
worshipping graven images.
we have refused to face
the dark truth that our civilisation
has become the greatest
threat to our civilisation.
we've become the very
worst enemies we have.
everything we did drove
us towards disaster.
if it hadn't been this
catastrophe it would've
been another.

we're overdue
an apocalypse. signs
are there in the culture.
we keep dreaming
about it, imagining it
in our novels,
poems, films, plays.
we're haunted by
an impending apocalypse
because deep down
we know we deserve it,
deep down we know
that we're racing
towards it with our deeds
and our dreams.

would it take a
true spiritual austerity
forced upon us to see
how bloated our
lives have become,
how empty, and how much
vanity and folly
we conceal from ourselves?

perhaps we travel too

much, polluting the skies
with restlessness
afraid to stay at home
quietly with those we
profess to love.

there's no need for panic.
for awareness is calm,
acts beyond emotion.

we tend to ramp
up the negatives,
multiply things we fear.
disaster sells.
it's a mysterious
thing about us
that we respond
much more to fear
than to goodness or love.
it's a human flaw
we ought to
compensate for.

a virus has entered
our mental sphere.
the plague is everywhere

it's in our dreams,
it's on tv,
from it we can't
be free.
it's a real contagion
a mental contagion.
it's destroying
us in nation after nation.
it's in the air we breathe
it's in the air we think.

a new contagion is needed
to fight the one that's seized
our lives. we need a contagion
of courage, health and love.
we need a new
spiritual condition
to fight our fears
fight our panic.

we seldom talk about
a healthy mind
a brave spirit
in our times of crisis.
the mind has its powers
the spirit has its mysteries

its miracles which surprise
the certainties of science.

for times like this
awaken the miraculous
in us. we're never more
ingenious than when we
act from solidarity.

we'll survive our
latest armageddon.
but we'll be marked
by how we got through it.
we will either be raised
by our courage
or degraded by our meanness.
here's the moment
to rise to the true potential
of our strength,
wisdom, farsightedness.

not just whether
we survive; it's also
who we become.
it's not just how we are
in prosperity that reveals us.

it's how we are when faced
with the ultimate test of all,
the test of death.
once a nation
during the great war rose
to the challenge
of character,
of destiny.
and her response
changed not only
herself but the world.

we're at such a turning
point in human history.
it was always coming for us.
disaster was always
coming for us.
we've overdrawn
on the bank
of our futures.
it's time to ask questions
that go all the way down
to the depths
of the meaning
of human life
the life of the species
the life of the earth.

our crisis is an opportunity
to change our destiny.
but the quality of that altering
depends on the best
lessons we take
from suffering.
sometimes we take
the worst lessons
from tragedy.
but we're transformed
most by those who
learned the best ones.

what has happened to us?
our books, art, plays
were measured not
by their inspiration
or how deeply they spoke
to us in the cage
of the human
but by how much
they sold for, how
many copies
were bought,
or how many lowered
their behinds on
the hardened seats.

we lost our way.
we lost the track, the path,
the road, altogether,
and are deep in the land
of moral vacuity,
spiritual emptiness.

we have been listening
to only one loud voice,
that speaks with the power
of a worldwide megaphone,
voice of profit,
gods of success.
so rigged are the goalposts
of values that other voices
are not heard.
they don't have great
social victories on their side
to prove universally strong
and persuasive. but does that
make them any less valuable?
voices that say they are
human too, and deserve
all the rights
of the human,
rights to health, to education,

to food, jobs, to raising
their families with dignity.
voices that speak
for climate crisis,
that speak not for raising
more walls but for a new
world co-operation.

we have entered the age
of disasters.
the age of narrowness
of heart is over. we
need to redirect our
values higher.

doctrines of hate
have nowhere to take us.
there's no real destiny
for limited dreams anymore.

we could be at the verge
of a miraculous moment
in which we deliberately
choose and fight for
an upward curve
in our evolutionary
possibilities. but

imagine what could happen to
the world if this crisis
brought about genuine
enlightenment
in our leaders,
in the people,
and if we pressed for change
at a time when we are most
vulnerable to death?

we are in potential
myth-making times.
it's time to make
a new myth for
humanity.
we could give birth
to a new kind of compassion,
new civic imagination,
new solidarity.
we're up to it.
it's why we fail so much,
fumble so much,
and keep clawing
our way back up,
keep moving the human
story further, through indirect,

circuitous ways. our
myths point in two
directions:
towards our fall,
towards our ascension.

that's the highest
meaning of tragedy.
time to listen.
time to ascend.

Invocation Hour

THE ANGLE

poet
sees life
a certain way.

nature
angle
relationship
to reality.

the master makes
something
out of nothing.

no such
thing as
nothing.

all things
imbued
with infinite
mystery
of origin.

mind shapes
the immortal
power
the atomic
reality.

BASED ON A TRANSLATION

i wander to the house of the one i love
where the plum tree brushes the eaves.
dripping with blossom and with leaves
the dew lies in the white flowers,
    lies there in the gentle hours.
i watch sparrows from the flower-cups drink.
singing of my love makes me think.

how do you go to your love's house?
    on the night-wind, with wings.
what calls you to your lover's house?
    everything fine that sings.
how many roads lead to your lover's house?
    more roads than sand.
which is the best road to your lover's house?
    all the roads in the land.

DIALLO'S TESTAMENT

Can you read the riddle of sense
In this portrait of me begun?
I am one on whom providence
Has worked its magic turn.
Behind me is a quivering story
Like a storm, or a stain.
As an African I have worn history
Round my neck like a chain.
I have sipped the language of death
I have shaped my canvas of earth.
I've crossed a sea of fires
And seen what not even empires
Nor great might can obscure.
Man is the sickness, God the cure.

THE ROHINGYAS

the hammer of
the army beats
down upon them
laws of the state
dispossess them
eagles that feed
on time's liver
devour them whole
and icons of justice
abandon them
they are scattered
in their thousands
across borders
and boundaries
and no one speaks for them
no one weeps at the rape of them
the laws say they cannot
buy land in their own lands
they're dispossessed
of citizenship in the place
where they are citizens.
they're the image
of powerlessness in
our time, the image of
vulnerability
of the peaceful way

in a time when
force moves
the world

and a religion
of light
dealing
darkness

on the edge of the world
where the centre
howls in its hollowness
a race of human beings
are perishing.
the world it seems
is good at being deaf.
the planet screams
women are raped
men are crushed
and tyranny
bursts at the seams
of its map and great powers
are silent. freedom's hand
bloody and broken
is compromised
by the feasting
on hearts in the towers.

it seems there are two worlds
in one pipelines
confer immunity
tanks and guns break
the flesh
in the other blood
runs fresh
skulls are broken
on the pavements of history.
nations preserve
their equanimity.
this silence is a mystery

can you watch a
man being flayed
alive in the open
wound of the street?
can you watch tanks
crush human feet?

and a religion
of peace
dealing
in agony?

this silence is a mystery.

BREATHING THE LIGHT

you died gently,
without fighting
what was murdering you.
and maybe that's
why your death moved
us so deeply. maybe
at the end there your life
seemed a wasted
thing, with three jail
terms behind you,
as you went to
the shop to buy
something with a
twenty-dollar
counterfeit bill.
the store owner
called the cops on
you, for twenty dollars.
i dread to think
how he must feel,
that his call in effect
led to your death.

we make too big a deal
about death.

it comes
and it's over.
it goes into the air,
into the earth.
it rarely changes life.

but all through that
last hour, as the
police manhandled you,
twisted your arm
behind your back,
forced you to the
ground, and one of
them, the weirdest
of them, stuck his
knee on your wind-
pipe and took no
notice as you
whispered something
sixteen times, the
two other officers
simply stood there,
witnesses to the law
killing the law,
while concerned citizens
attempt intervention,
without power.

you didn't see all
that. maybe all you saw
were the final moments
of your leap, when
on the school team,
you were going to touch
the sky and touch
the world; your leap
back then, how full
of promise, full
of the power to help
a team win. life
afterwards was a long
fall into the abyss
of america, where
to be black is to make
an early pact
with death, not your
own death, but the death
that's waiting for you in
the blackness of
america.

maybe you saw all that
or remembered you at
a friend's wedding

wearing a white suit, tall
like the bridegroom of
aphrodite, tall for
a big destiny, that
eluded you,
year after year,
in the purple
light of the republic.

and all those roads,
all those failed prom-
ises brought you
here, with your neck
beneath the knee
of a policeman,
the breath of life
fading from you
like the fragrance
from the autumn roses.
you called your breath
sixteen times, like
a sad lover, while two
white women filmed
the grim catastrophe
of injustice that bloomed
there in lincoln's

graveyard, the whole
broken earth of
america.

you didn't fight
you simply faded as
your breath drifted
away beneath
the knee of justice.
you hadn't been charged
you hadn't been tried
you hadn't been found guilty.
you had not been sentenced
and yet you were
being crushed to
death, while
the whole
world watched.

maybe it's because you
did not fight, did
not struggle, because you
knew that to resist was
to invite death
from the law. you
learned not to struggle, not

to curse, not to protest,
not to fight back, only
how to die like flotsam
on a receding tide.
it was a kind of love,
your dying. a kind of
gentleness. There's
no end to the insult
we suffer. when
did it really begin?

but it was that
way you let your
breath go, let it
go sixteen times,
watching it, eyes
slowly dimming,
maybe it was
your doing nothing but
let the heart of
america reveal
itself that was
the greatest way
of speaking, the
greater way of
dying, that brings

down the whole dead
house of race, that
died long ago
in white power,
in black silence,
died but did not
know it, because
of all the guns,
the law, the whole
invisible, inviolate
matrix of sustenance.

but hatred dies
slowly, dies a long time
and maybe will never
die truly as long as
eyes see fear where
heart sees flowers.
what did i ever do
to be hated by you?

and so your death
passed into the
force of history,
because it awakened
the silences

the pain
the injustices that
have been stored up
for four hundred
colourless years.

you died into silence
but the big world
rose up in speech.

there's no poetry
of change greater
than when the world
sees at last that
it can be free

free to breathe the light that
keeps the republic alive.

INVOCATION FOR THE SHRINE 4

revelations come fast
with harvests of spirits.
for the world is not as it seems.
free yourselves from the illusion of limits.

here are the miracles unseen
time turning the limits of the past
into wise new freedom. redream
chains into fires that last.

saint time speaks from the shrine
of the hours; speaks about the powers
of the blacks who are free and can dream
free to weave power from flowers.

bring a clear dream for the world
you who walk this way. bring your light.
bring your wisdom, your fire, your hope.
bring a new courage, a new fight.

LINES TOWARDS A LOVE POEM

a voice in the flower.
and i am missing you.
on the edge of anguish.

hey, light-thrower,

i'm throwing love your way.

pure form
and luminous spirit,
beyond the body you
distil pleasures.

kissing you stops
time and the mind.
i carry you in me
like a poem unread,
a classic song,
or that full moon.

i am craving your gaze.
just a long kiss
without breathing.

so be patient.
let love and time
do their mysterious work.

i woke with a new clarity.
we earn what life will give
us, earn it with courage,
love and wisdom.
i'm sending you my tears
to open your way.

sow your talent

reap your genius.

GRENFELL TOWER, JUNE 2017

It was like a burnt matchbox in the sky.
It was black and long and burnt in the sky.
You saw it through flowering stumps of trees.
You saw it beyond the ochre spire of the church.
You saw it in the tears of those who survived.
You saw it through the rage of those who survived.
You saw it past the posters of those who burnt to
    ashes.
You saw it past the posters of those who jumped to
    their deaths.
You saw it through TV images of flames through
    windows
Running up the aluminium cladding
You saw it in print images of flames bursting out
    from the roof.
You heard it in voices loud in the streets.
You heard it in cries in the air howling for justice.
You heard it in pubs streets basements dives.
You heard it in wailing of women and silent screams
Of orphans wandering the streets
You saw it in your baby who couldn't sleep at night
Spooked by ghosts that wander the area still trying
To escape fires that came at them black and
    choking.
You saw it in dreams of the dead who asked if living
Has no meaning being poor in a land

Where the poor die in flames without warning.
But when you saw it with your eyes it seemed what
the eyes
Saw didn't make sense can't make sense won't
make sense.
You saw it there in the sky, tall and black and burnt.
You counted the windows, counted the floors
And saw the sickly yellow of half-burnt cladding
And what you saw could only be seen in nightmare.
Like a warzone in a fashionable borough.
A warzone planted here in the city.
To see with the eyes that which one only sees
In nightmares turns the day to night, turns the
world upside down.

Those who were living now are dead
Those who were breathing are from the living earth
fled.
If you want to see how the poor die, come see
Grenfell Tower.
See the tower, and let a world-changing dream flower.

Residents of the area call it the crematorium.
It has revealed the undercurrents of our age.
The poor who thought voting for the rich would
save them.

The poor who believed all that the papers said.
The poor who listened with their fears.
The poor who live in their rooms and dream for
    their kids.
The poor are you and I, you in your garden of
    flowers,
In your house of books, who gaze from afar
At a destiny that draws near with another name.
Sometimes it takes an image to wake a nation
From its secret shame. And here it is every name
Of someone burnt to death, on the stairs or in their
    room,
Who had no idea what they died for, or how they
    were betrayed.
They did not die when they died; their deaths
    happened long
Before. Happened in the minds of people who never
    saw
Them. It happened in the profit margins.
    Happened
In the laws. They died because money could be
    saved and made.

Those who are living now are dead
Those who were breathing are from the living earth
    fled.

If you want to see how the poor die, come see
    Grenfell Tower
See the tower, and let a world-changing dream flower.

They called the tower ugly; dubbed it an eyesore.
All around the beautiful people in their beautiful
    houses
Didn't want the ugly tower to ruin their house
    prices.
Ten million was spent to encase the tower in
    cladding.
Had it ever been tested before except upon this
    eyesore,
Had it ever been tested for fire, been tried in a blaze?
But it made the tower look pretty, yes it made the
    tower look pretty.
But in twenty-four storeys, not a single sprinkler.
In twenty-four storeys not a single alarm that worked.
Twenty-four storeys not a single fire escape,
Only a dank stairwell designed in hell, waiting
For an inferno. That's the story of our times.
Make it pretty on the outside, a death trap
On the inside. Make the hollow sound nice, make
The empty look good. That's all they will see,
How it looks, how it sounds, not how it really is,
    unseen.

But if you really look you can see it, if you really
    listen
You can hear it. Got to look beneath the cladding.
There's cladding everywhere. Political cladding,
Economic cladding, intellectual cladding – things
    that look good
But have no centre, have no heart, only moral
    padding.
They say the words but the words are hollow.
They make the gestures, and the gestures are
    shallow.
Their bodies come to the burnt tower, but their
    souls don't follow.

Those who were living are now dead.
Those who were breathing are from the living earth
    fled.
If you want to see how the poor die, come see
    Grenfell Tower.
See the tower, and let a world-changing deed flower.

The voices here must speak for the dead.
Speak for the dead. Speak for the dead.
See their pictures line the walls. Poverty is its own
Colour, its own race. They were Muslim and
    Christian,

Black and white and colours in between. They were
	young
And old, beautiful and middle-aged. There were
	girls
In their best dresses, hearts open to the future.
There was an old man with his grandchildren;
There was Kadija, a young artist,
There was Amaya Tuccu, three years old,
Burnt to ashes before she could see the lies of the
	world.
There are names who were living beings who dreamt
Of fame or contentment, education or love
Who are now ashes in a burnt-out shell of cynicism.
There were two Italians, lovely and young,
Who in the inferno were on their mobile phone to
	friends
When the smoke of profits suffocated their voices.
There was the baby thrown from many storeys high
By a mother who knew otherwise he would die.
There were those who jumped from windows,
Those who died because they were told to stay
In their burning rooms. There was the little girl on
	fire
Seen leaping from the twentieth floor. Need I say
	more.

Those who are living are now dead
Those who were breathing are from the living earth
   fled.
If you want to see how the poor die, come see
   Grenfell Tower.
See the tower, and let a world-altering deed flower.

Always there's that discrepancy
Between what happens and what we are told.
Official figures were stuck at thirty.
But truth in the world is rarer than gold.
Bodies brought out in the dark
Bodies still in the dark.
Dark the smoke, dark the head.
Those who were living are now dead.

And while the tower flamed they were tripping
Over bodies at the stairs
Because it was pitch black.
Those that survived
Slept like refugees on the floor
Of a sports centre.
And like creatures scared of the dark,
A figure from on high flits by,
Speaking to the police and firefighters,
But then avoiding the victims,

Whose hearts must be brimming with dread.
*Those who were breathing are from the living earth
fled.*

But if you go to Grenfell Tower, that's if you can pull
Yourselves from your tennis games and perfect
dinners,
If you go there while the black skeleton of that living
tower
Still stands unreal in the air, a warning for other
towers to fear,
You will breathe the air thick with grief
Women spontaneously weeping
Children wandering around stunned
Men secretly wiping a tear from the eye
And people unbelieving staring at this sinister form
in the sky
You'll see the trees, their leaves clean and green
And you'll inhale the incense meant
To cleanse the air of its unhappiness
You'll see banks of flowers
And white papered walls sobbing with condolences
And candles burning for the blessing of the dead
You will see the true meaning of community
Food shared, stories told and volunteers
everywhere;

You'll breathe the air of incinerators
All mixed with the essence of life's flower.
If you want to see how the poor die, see
    Grenfell Tower.

Make sense of these figures if you will
For the spirit lives where truth can't kill.
Ten million spent on the falsely clad
In a fire where hundreds lost all they had.
Five million offered in relief
Should make a nation alter its belief.
An image gives life and an image kills.
But the heart reveals itself beyond political skills.
In this age of austerity
The poor die for others' prosperity.
Nurseries and libraries fade from the land.
A strange time is shaping on the strand.
Swords of fate hang over the deafness of power.
See the tower, and let a new world-changing
    thought flower.

WALK IN A MOONLIGHT WONDER

walk in a moon
light wonder; white
houses on cliffs
of a magic sea.
the sky drowning
in blue; the white
stones turn
red and yellow
and brown
in the solitary stretch
of the breathing land.

woman walking
in black across
the henna-coloured
earth. a green dog
on a black leash sent
from a wandering
mind. one of the dog's
legs is blue in
drenching moonlight.
she is draped all
in black. splendour
of black in the brilliance
of the dreaming walk

in a moonlight wonder.